THE ESCAPADES OF CLINT M^cCOOL

OCTO-MAN AND THE HEADLESS MONSTER

by Jane Kelley
illustrated by Jessika von Innerebner

Grosset & Dunlap
An Imprint of Penguin Random House

GROSSET & DUNLAP
Penguin Young Readers Group
An Imprint of Penguin Random House LLC

Text copyright © 2017 by Jane Kelley. Illustrations copyright © 2017
by Penguin Random House LLC. All rights reserved. Published
by Grosset & Dunlap, an imprint of Penguin Random House LLC,
345 Hudson Street, New York, New York 10014. GROSSET & DUNLAP is
a trademark of Penguin Random House LLC. Manufactured in China.

Library of Congress Cataloging-in-Publication Data is available.

ISBN 9780448487533 (paperback)   10 9 8 7 6 5 4 3 2 1
ISBN 9780448487540 (library binding)   10 9 8 7 6 5 4 3 2 1

For my husband, Lee, whose
great ideas always save the day—JK

To everyone who's had a crazy idea
and the courage to run with it—JVI

1

CLINT McCOOL NEEDS HIS CAP

The clock ticks. Our teacher, Ms. Apple, talks. Kids multiply the sevens. Everything seems normal. But you can't fool Clint McCool. I know we're trapped here. And I know why. Someone doesn't want school to end. The big hand of the clock is stuck. It can't get to the twelve.

"Break free," I whisper to the big hand.

Ms. Apple frowns at me. She thinks I'm not paying attention. But I'm the only one who is!

I tap my finger. Nothing happens. Rats. My Speed Accelerator won't work unless I push the right button on my cap. Marco made the buttons for me. He's very clever. That's why he's the best best friend ever. The buttons are amazing. They always help me save the day. That has to happen more than you'd think.

But I can't wear my cap in school. Ms. Apple keeps it locked in her desk. My Laser

Beam could cut a hole in the drawer. But its button is on the cap, too. How can Clint McCool save the day?

Zing, zong, zing. Brain flash! I jump up. "I need a remote!"

"Walter, sit down," Ms. Apple says.

That's right. She called me Walter. My parents named me after my grandpa. Luckily, Clint McCool decided to name himself.

I sit—on the edge of my chair. I stay ready for action. I wiggle my ears to send a message to Marco. He's writing. Oh no. Is he doing math problems?

I crinkle my nose to send a message to M.L. Her real name is Magnolia Lynn. No one dares to call her that. Not even her own mother.

M.L. is writing, too. Did those sevens take over my friends' brains? How can we have an escapade? M.L. and Marco are coming home with me today. School better end soon. My

friends are forgetting how to have fun.

Finally, the bell rings. Kids get in line. I rush to Ms. Apple's desk to get my cap.

Ms. Apple won't give it to me. "I need to talk to your mother, Walter."

I'm doomed.

Ms. Apple leads us to the school yard. The adults are waiting there. Mom smiles at me and my friends. She looks happy. Until Ms. Apple starts talking to her.

"Ready for an escapade, Clint McCool?" Marco asks.

That's another reason he's my best friend. He calls me by my real name.

"Will your mom take us to the park?" M.L. says.

"I drew a map of where the Gronks hid the treasure." Marco opens up his notebook.

M.L. and I look. Marco did a great job. Especially with the crocodiles in the moat.

"At the top of the tower? Let's go!" M.L. says.

She loves to climb. That's why she hates wearing dresses. The fluff gets in her way.

"Before the Gronks know we're coming!" Marco says.

I run to get Mom.

"Walter isn't a bad boy," Mom is telling Ms. Apple.

"He doesn't follow rules. He can't sit still," Ms. Apple says. "He never thinks before he acts."

"I'm always thinking," I interrupt. "Aren't ideas thinking?"

"You shouldn't have ideas like that at school." Ms. Apple gives the cap to Mom—not me. "Remember what I said will happen if Walter doesn't improve."

Mom, Marco, M.L., and I leave the school yard. We walk along Eighth Avenue.

"What did Ms. Apple mean?" I try to get my cap. I need the Translator button. Grown-ups can be hard to understand. "What's wrong with my ideas?"

We turn the corner at Twelfth
Street.

Mom sighs. "You have so many."

"Isn't that a good thing?" I say.

"Is Clint McCool in trouble?" Marco says.

"If Walter can't behave, they'll find ways to make him," Mom says.

I gulp. "What kind of ways?"

"Ways," Mom says again.

"I could make him a new button," Marco says.

"I could keep him safe." M.L. locks her arms around me.

She's strong. But I'm slippery.

I break free. I run ahead.

A man blocks the sidewalk with his arm. "Please wait here."

I can't! M.L. will catch me. I run along Twelfth Street.

"Walter! This isn't behaving!" Mom yells.

I run faster.

Then I stop.

A monster stands right in front of me. His head is an octopus. It oozes slime and ink.

I rub my eyes. I still see the monster. He carries a jar full of brains.

I scream. So does everybody else.

"Get away from Octo-Man!" I hear the man shout.

Octo-Man staggers toward me.

Oh no! Are these the ways
Ms. Apple meant?

2

BANNED FROM THE SET!

Octo-Man skids to a stop right in front of me.

Big cameras are pointed at Octo-Man.

"Cut! Cut! Set up the scene again," another man says.

Now I get it. These people are making a movie.

Octo-Man's head is a costume.

I wonder if Marco could make us one.
I squeeze one of the arms. It breaks
off in my hands.

People gasp. "Oh no! Octo-Man is
ruined!"

A bald man snatches the arm
away from me. "Look what you did!"

Why is everyone upset? It's just an
arm. Octo-Man has seven others.

Mom rushes over. "I'm very sorry.

It was an accident. We're going home now."

Mom puts her arm around my shoulders. That isn't a hug. That's how she steers me. We walk toward Ninth Avenue. Marco and M.L. follow us. Mom gives me back my cap. Marco straightens it. M.L. pulls it down over my eyes.

Another guard stands at the corner of Ninth Avenue. After we pass him, I turn around. He blocks the sidewalk with his whole body.

I try to see the movie people. A redheaded lady sews the arm back on Octo-Man.

"You better move on," the guard says.

"Can't we watch from here?" M.L. asks.

"No," the guard says.

"We won't go on the set," Marco says.

"We promise," I say.

The guard frowns at me. So do Marco and M.L. They think it's my fault they can't stay.

"Come on, kids. Let's go home," Mom says.

Go home? We can't go home! There aren't any monsters in our apartment.

Mom takes my hand like I'm a two-year-old. Is this the end? Has Clint McCool been defeated? No, wait. I can still save the day. I'm wearing my cap!

Hmmm. Which button should
I use? The Reverse Time-O-Meter?
I can go back to before the arm broke.
I start to push the button. Then I stop.
I'd better be careful. I might go all the
way back to school.

"Oh no!" the bald man shouts.

We all look. Octo-Man's arm fell off
again.

"Does anyone know how to fix this?" the bald man asks.

I do!

I run around the guard onto the movie set. "I can help! Clint McCool will save the day."

I push the Idea Generator. *Zing, zong, zing.* Brain flash!

"Tie it on. With a bloody bandage. Give him a pirate hook. Just get rid of it. Why does he need eight arms? Maybe he lost one in a fight." I swing my arms at Octo-Man.

The bald man crouches down and grabs my shoulders. "You want to help?"

"Of course I do! Isn't that what I said?" I fix my cap. I'm ready. "What do you want me to do?"

"Stay away from the set," the bald man says.

Hmmm. How will that help? Why do grown-ups talk in code? I push the Translator button on my cap. "What do you mean 'stay away'?"

"Get out of here! Scram! Keep off the set!" the bald man yells.

3

A New ESCAPADE?

Mom grabs my hand again. We walk to the corner.

"I'd better take Marco and M.L. home," Mom says.

"No!" we shout.

"You got in enough trouble already," Mom says.

What Mom calls *trouble* is usually an escapade. This could be the best one ever. What could top seeing Octo-Man make a movie? Nothing except . . .

Zing, zong, zing. Brain flash! If Clint McCool were in the movie!

I'm so excited, I jump up and down.

"What's gotten into you?" Mom says.

I can't say. Mom shouldn't find out my ideas—until it's too late.

I push the Face Changing button. I need to look serious. "I just remembered. We have homework."

MESSAGE
TRANSMISSION

"What?" Marco and M.L. look at me.

I push the Message Transmission button.

"Oh. That homework," Marco says.

"Okay," Mom says, "but just for thirty minutes. I have to cook dinner and finish up some paperwork. Walter? Are you listening?"

Actually, I'm not. If Mom wants me to, she should talk about something interesting.

"Never mind." Mom stomps into our building.

Marco, M.L., and I follow her up the stairs.

"Your mom seems mad," Marco says.

"Don't worry. She won't be for long," I say.

"How do you know?" M.L. says.

"There's a secret weapon in our apartment," I say.

Mom unlocks the door. A yellow beast gallops over. He licks Mom's face.

It's Hercules, our dog. He has

special powers, too. His slobber
always makes Mom smile.

"We go into my bedroom.

"What's up, Clint McCool?" Marco
says.

"I'm going to be in that movie,"
I say.

"But you're banned from the set,"
Marco says.

"So are we. And I wanted to watch

Octo-Man," M.L. says.

"You can. We just need to get past the guard," I say.

Marco and M.L. look at each other.

"Can't you think of another escapade?" Marco says.

"Where we could have fun?" M.L. adds.

"And not get into trouble?" they both say together.

"That movie needs Clint McCool. Then I won't get yelled at for having ideas," I say.

"They don't want your help. That bald man was really mad," Marco says.

"Let's hunt for treasure like we planned," M.L. says.

Marco takes out his notebook. He opens it to the map. I see a tunnel under the fort.

Zing, zong, zing. Brain flash! "I know. We could crawl through an underground pipe and pop up in the middle of Twelfth Street," I say.

"How can you get into the pipe?" Marco says.

TUNNEL

"M.L.'s strong. She can dig a hole,"
I say.

"With what?" M.L. says.

I look under my bed. That's where
I keep my supplies. I find an apple
core and an empty toilet
paper tube.

M.L. laughs.

I frown. I have
to find a way
underground.

Zing, zong, zing.
Brain flash! "I know how to get in."

I run to the bathroom. I put my
foot in the toilet.

"Walter, what are you doing?"
Mom says.

"Washing my shoe?" I say.

Mom crosses her arms. She doesn't
speak. Her lips are squeezed together
tight.

I take my foot out of the toilet. It
drips.

"It's time to take your friends
home. I need to walk Hercules,"
Mom says.

"Not yet!" I take off my shoe. I hop back to my room. I have to find a way past the guard.

I push the Idea Generator. Oops. Wrong button. Instead of ideas, I get dance moves.

Hercules barks. M.L. dances with me. Marco cheers. "That's brilliant, Clint McCool!"

Zing, zong, zing. Brain flash!
"I know why the movie people sent
me away. They thought I was just
a kid. They don't know I can do
amazing things. There's just one
problem," I say.

"Only one?" M.L. says.

"Choosing the best thing! Should
I walk on my hands? Should I juggle?
Should I ride a horse down Twelfth
Street?" I say.

"Walter!" Mom calls. "Time to go!"

I run into the kitchen. "Mom,
I need more time."

Mom gets something out of the
refrigerator. "I told you. I have to walk
Hercules right now. And then I have
to cook dinner."

I gasp when I see what she's
holding.

Zing, zong, zing. Brain flash!

It's the perfect thing to get me in
the movie! Best of all, I won't need
a horse.

4

CLINT McCOOL IS A MONSTER?

I *grab the cauliflower* from Mom.

"What are you doing?" Mom says.

"Marco and M.L. need a snack," I say.

"Wouldn't they rather have cookies?" Mom says.

"You always say to eat more vegetables."

I take the cauliflower into my room. "I can just walk past the guard. He won't know it's me," I say.

"You know the Invisibility button doesn't totally work," Marco says.

I hold up the cauliflower.

"Is that to bribe the guard?" M.L. asks.

"No. Doesn't this look like brains?"

I balance the cauliflower on my head. It falls on the floor.

Hercules sniffs it.

"You lost your head." Marco laughs.

M.L. picks up the cauliflower. "Heads-up." She throws it at Marco.

"Don't get a*head* of yourself." Marco laughs.

I grab the cauliflower. "We don't have time for jokes."

"Or snacks. Or fun," M.L. says.

I ignore her. I put the cauliflower back on my head. "These are my extra brains. Now I look like an actor in the movie. Right?"

"Maybe," Marco says.

"It won't stay," M.L. says.

I let go. It falls.

M.L. catches the cauliflower.

I take it back from her. "Marco, can you make some glue that looks like dripping blood?"

Marco shakes his head.

"You have to help me be a monster," I say.

"I think you already are one," M.L. says.

Hmmm. Is that a compliment?

I put the cauliflower back on my head. "I'll just hold it."

"You need to cover up your hands," Marco says.

"And your face," M.L. says.

I pull my shirt up to my forehead. "How does this look?" I say.

I hear laughing.

Hmmm. I must need a better shirt. I take off my shirt.

Marco's shirt has a skeleton. I put down the cauliflower and tug at Marco's shirt.

"What are you doing?" M.L. says.

"Marco's shirt looks scarier," I say.

"But it's my favorite shirt," Marco says.

"I'll give it right back," I say.

"Walter? Let's go!" Mom calls.

"Why won't you help me?" I ask.

"Why should we help you get in trouble?" Marco says.

"I won't. It's the best escapade ever," I say.

Marco and I trade shirts. I put the cauliflower back on my head. I stagger around. I need to make noises. But what kind? Would a

monster with extra brains groan?
Gurgle? Rasp? Gurgle-rasp?

"Arggggh, blergggle, arggggh,"
I say.

Mom knocks on the door. "Are you
okay, Walter?"

"Yes. We're just finishing our
snack," I say.

I put the cauliflower in M.L.'s

backpack. I try to zip it. The zipper gets stuck. I yank at the tab. M.L. grabs it from me. "Stop. You'll rip it."

Mom comes into the room.

Marco and M.L. are frowning. Hmmm. I wonder why. I don't have time to worry about them. We need to hurry.

"Do you want a snack that isn't cauliflower?" Mom says.

"No, thank you," Marco says.

"We want to go home," M.L. says.

Mom looks puzzled. "Okay. Are you ready, Walter?"

I think about what I need. Plan? Yes. Gurgle? Yes. Monster head? Yes.

Clint McCool is ready to be in the movies!

5

TROUBLE ON TWELFTH STREET

Mom puts the leash on Hercules. He barks. He licks Mom's face again.

I forgot Hercules is coming, too. This is terrible! Dogs don't know how to be in a movie. What if he jumps on me? What if he knocks off my monster head? What if he goes wild chasing pigeons? You never know what a dog will do.

Hercules pulls Mom down the street. I hurry after them. Marco and M.L. follow. I hear them whispering. It's okay. They'll stop being mad at me after I'm in the movie. They'll think it's cool, having a movie-star best friend.

We're on Twelfth Street. I can see Octo-Man. His eighth arm is taped on. The bald man hands Octo-Man the jar of brains. I'm so excited.

The guard walks toward us. Oh no! He'll send me away before I can put on my disguise! I push my Invisibility button. Three times! Nothing happens.

The guard comes closer. Does he see me?

I hide behind Hercules. Hercules won't stand still! I hold his collar. My hand gets tangled in the leash. The leash comes off. Hercules runs toward a food table.

"Hercules! Come back!" Mom shouts.

Mom and the guard chase after him.

What a good dog! Now's my chance. I take the cauliflower out of M.L.'s backpack.

"Are you sure you want to do this?" M.L. says.

I hand my cap to Marco.

"You might need those buttons," Marco says.

"Nope. I'll be great!" I grab the cauliflower by its leaves. I pull Marco's shirt over my face. I hold it up with my teeth.

On the outside, I look calm—for a monster. Inside, I'm jumping with excitement.

I hear Mom say, "Thank you for catching Hercules."

"No problem," the guard says.

Then Mom says, "Let's go, kids. Wait. Where's Walter?"

Walter has disappeared! A dangerous monster with extra brains staggers down Twelfth Street. "Arggggh, blergggle, arggggh."

"Walter! Come back here!"

Is Mom shouting? I can't hear

much inside the shirt—except my gurgling noises. "Argghh, blergggle, argghh."

I hear more shouting. But I don't hear people screaming with terror and delight.

Hmmm. Maybe I need to be scarier. I wiggle the cauliflower. I hear something snap. The leaves break. The cauliflower falls off my head. It rolls down the street.

I chase after my brain. I wave my arms. They wouldn't know what to do if they lost their brain. My legs are kicking, too. This is brilliant! My whole body is out of control. The guard can't grab me.

I pick up the cauliflower. I put my

brain back on my head. I say, "Nine times nine is eighty-one." That's the smartest thing I can think of at the moment.

There's Octo-Man. I lurch toward him. "Scrrrump trozzle pluuuuu?"

That means *Nice to meet you* in monster talk.

Before Octo-Man can answer, the

guard grabs me by the back of the shirt.

I try to pull away. I have to get to Octo-Man. The shirt rips. I fall forward. I crash into Octo-Man. He drops the jar. Glass breaks. His brains ooze all over the sidewalk.

Everybody screams. It's totally amazing.

RRiiip

"Walter, what have you done?" Mom shrieks.

I'm lying on the sidewalk. I can't believe it. Usually, my plans get out of control. But this time, they didn't. It happened just like I imagined.

"No, no, no!" the bald man shouts.

Why is he mad? Did they run out of film? Do I need to do it again?

I jump up. I'm ready.

The bald man stares at me for a moment. Then he shouts, "Get that kid out of here!"

CLINT McCOOL SAVES THE DAY?!?

6

The bald man kicks the cauliflower. Mom rushes over. "Walter didn't mean to cause so much trouble."

"I told you to stay away! You broke the jar! The brain is ruined! The movie is ruined!" the bald man shouts.

"Come on, Walter," Mom says. "We have to take Marco and M.L. home."

I shake my head. I don't want my friends to leave.

Marco and M.L. are staring at my shoulder. I look down. Marco's favorite shirt is ripped.

I feel terrible. I wanted to be in the movie. But I ruined it. For everybody. I look at all the sad faces. Octo-Man's eight arms all droop.

Now I really need to save the day. But my cap won't help. I can't do anything. Except say I'm sorry.

I walk over to the bald man. "I'm sorry I ruined your movie. I didn't mean to. I just wanted to be part of it. I love the monster you made. Octo-Man is still amazing. Even without the brain in a jar."

"He has to steal something," the bald man says.

"Monsters don't care about brains. Can't he steal something else?" I say.

"Like what? A cauliflower?" the bald man says.

I shrug. I don't know.

Mom gives me a hug. It feels really good. Now I have to apologize to Marco and M.L. Saying you're sorry is much harder than all the other ways Clint McCool usually has to save the day.

I walk toward my friends.

Marco and M.L. won't even look at me. I guess their shoes are doing something interesting.

I twist the ripped shirt. I want them to be my friends again. More than anything.

Zing, zong, zing. Brain flash!

I run back to the bald man. "I know what Octo-Man wants: friends."

"Friends?"

"You know, people to like him. No matter if he messes up. Which he shouldn't. But sometimes he does."

The bald man doesn't say anything. He frowns.

I guess he's still mad. I want to tell Marco and M.L. what I just figured out. I walk over to them.

The bald man yells, "Hey! Kid.

Where do you think you're going?"

I can't believe I'm in trouble again! Well, actually I can, since I usually am.

"Come back here!" the bald man shouts.

I walk toward him slowly.

What kind of punishment can he give me? He isn't my teacher. He can't give me more homework. He isn't my mom. He can't make me eat the cauliflower.

I walk past the brain on the sidewalk. I think it's fake. Or did

it come from a kid with too many ideas?

"Walter said he was sorry," Mom says.

"I know. But what about my movie?" The bald man points at me. "I know all about you. You'd do anything to make life more exciting. Wouldn't you?"

My head wobbles yes.

"I knew a kid just like you. He always got in trouble. He had too many ideas. Do you know what happened to him?"

I shake my head.

He swings his arm around. His finger points at the brain on the sidewalk.

I gasp. Oh no! I was right! They did get the brain from a kid.

But his arm keeps moving. It stops when he points at himself.

7

CLINT McCOOL IN THE MOVIES??

"*You were like me?*" I say.

"Real life is boring sometimes," he whispers to me.

We both laugh.

Then he gets serious. "People like us have tons of ideas. That's the easy part. But when you make movies, you have to focus on one idea."

"Just one? No zinging?" I say.

"Not all the time. Or you won't get anything done. Don't let your ideas run wild. Be their boss. Can you do that?"

I nod. "I can try."

"Good. Because you're right. Octo-Man would want a friend."

"A grown-up likes my idea?" I stagger backward.

The bald man catches me. "Would you like to be that friend?"

I gulp. Me? Be the friend? In the movie? "You mean it?"

"Yes. We want contrast! We want surprise! And that will be you." He shakes my hand. "My name is Sam. I'm the director. You have to listen to me. Can you do that?"

"Yes," I squeak. I can hardly talk. I squeeze my head. It zings so much. I feel like I really do have extra brains.

"Great. Now we'd better ask your mom."

"MOM!" I run over to her. Sam follows.

She's standing with Marco, M.L., and Hercules. "Can I take my son home now?"

"I've got something he needs to do." Sam talks to Mom. Mom looks shocked.

"Are you done getting yelled at?"
M.L. says.

"No. I mean, yes," I say.

Mom signs some papers.

"What's going on, Clint McCool?"
Marco says.

"Is your mom sending you away?"
M.L. says.

Sam grabs my arm. "Come on, kid.
We're losing our light. You've got one
chance to get it right."

"You kids wait here with the
guard. I have to go with Walter,"
Mom says.

"Wait! Where are you taking Clint
McCool?" Marco says.

"Don't worry." I wave at Marco and
M.L. Hercules barks.

Sam, Mom, and I walk up some stairs. We go inside a building.

Movie people are sitting around. Octo-Man's head is on the floor. He stands up when we come in. "Not him again."

"Change in plans," Sam says. "Jim, you're going to steal the kid. Can you pick him up?"

Octo-Man lifts me up.

"Great. How about some wriggling and screaming?" Sam says to me.

I flail my arms. I shriek like I'm covered in hot lava.

"How about less wriggling and screaming?" Sam says.

How could he want less? Then I get it. Clint McCool would be brave. We try it again. I flap my arms and shout, "Eek!"

"Perfect. Now you need a costume," Sam says.

We follow a redheaded woman into another room.

"Should I get the cauliflower?"
I say.

They laugh. Hmmm. It probably
is dirty.

There's a rack full of clothes and
masks. Octo-Man's friend will be a
monster. But what kind?

One rubber head has dangling eyeballs. One has oozing scars. One is a giant fly face. It's really gross. I hope I'll wear it.

"I got it!" the redheaded woman says.

Sam goes over to the rack.

"Yes! He's going to be adorable."

Adorable? Hmmm. What kind of monster is that? I wish I had my cap. I need to push the Translator button.

"Help him get changed," Sam says to Mom. "We'll shoot the scene as soon as he's ready."

The redheaded woman holds up a costume.

I gasp. It's the scariest thing I've ever seen—a pink polka-dot dress.

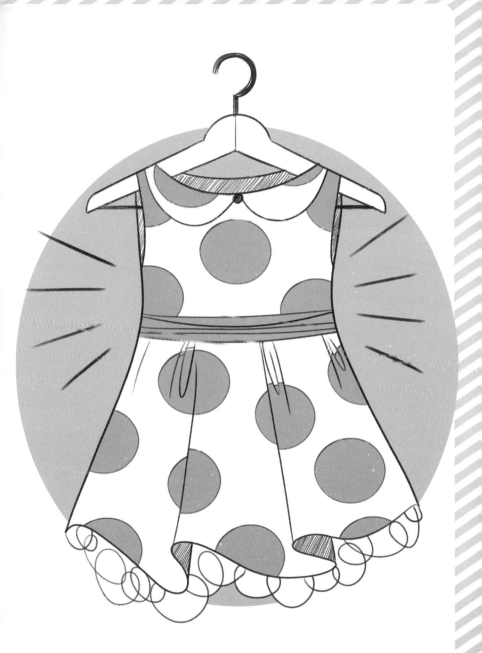

8

DON'T BE SCARED OF A DRESS!

The redheaded woman holds up the dress. "This should fit."

I have to get away from the pink! I stagger backward. I bump into the rack. It crashes to the ground.

"I guess Walter changed his mind," Mom says.

"Don't you want to be in the movie?" Sam asks.

"Yes. But I have a new idea. I'm not Octo-Man's friend. I'm a monster fighter named Clint McCool. I have a special cap. With buttons for all my superpowers."

Sam squats down and looks into my eyes. "What did I say about ideas?"

"Find one. And stick to it," I say.

"Who's the boss?" Sam says.

"You are," I say.

"Yes. But you are, too. Can you do it?" Sam says. "Can you save the movie?"

I think about it. Then I nod.

Mom helps me put on the pink dress. And a hat. With ribbons. And a daisy on top.

When I'm ready, Octo-Man and I stand in the hall by the front door.

We wait quietly for Sam's signal to run outside. We wait. And wait.

The dress itches. My heart pounds.

My brain zings like crazy.

But I don't move. I don't talk.
I don't even make monster noises.

How can I stand still? I don't have
my cap. I just keep telling myself,
Don't mess up this movie!

The pink oozes into me. My skin burns. My bones wobble. I tell myself, *Don't mess up this movie!* What if I mess up this movie? MESS UP THIS MOVIE!?!!?!

No! I won't! Clint McCool can be the boss of himself and save the movie!

"Action!" Sam shouts.

Octo-Man picks me up. The door opens. I wriggle and squeal. Octo-Man carries me down the steps and along Twelfth Street.

"Cut!" Sam shouts.

Octo-Man puts me down. "Did you get the shot?"

"Good job, everyone. You got it right on the first try!" Sam shouts.

I run back inside the building. I rip off the hat and the dress. I put on Marco's shirt. I'm myself again.

I go over to where Mom and my friends are waiting. Hercules wags his tail. He's glad to see me. Marco and M.L. look worried. Marco gives me back my cap.

"Why were you in that building?" Marco says.

"Did they lock you up while they finished the movie?" M.L. asks.

"No. My idea saved the day." I grin. "So I was in the movie."

"What?" Marco says.

"How?" M.L. says.

"I told Sam that Octo-Man should steal a friend. Even monsters want friends," I say.

"That's really smart," Marco says.

"How did you think of that?" M.L. says.

"Because I know I need my friends," I say. "I'm sorry I ripped your shirt, Marco. I'm sorry I didn't listen to you, M.L."

"That's okay," Marco and M.L. say.

"No, it isn't. I'm going to do better. You deserve better. You guys are the best!" I say.

M.L. punches me in the arm. I punch her back. Marco bonks us with his notebook. We're friends again.

"But, Clint McCool, you said you were in the movie," Marco says.

"I was," I say.

"We didn't see you," M.L. says.

"Octo-Man carried a girl down the street," Marco says.

M.L.'s eyes get really big. Her smile gets even bigger. She whispers to Marco.

His glasses fall off. "No way," he says.

"Yes. That was Walter. Wearing a dress. That was pink!" M.L. laughs.

I laugh, too. "Who cares? Clint McCool has defeated a zillion enemies. He can't be scared of a dress."

Sam the director comes over. He shakes my hand. "Good job, kid."

"These are my friends. They gave

me the idea," I say.

"Thanks, kids. That idea saved the movie," Sam says.

"Clint McCool saved the movie!" Marco shouts.

Everybody shouts, "Hooray!" Hercules barks. Mom cheers loudest of all.

Clint McCool tips his cap. He doesn't brag about saving the day.

But my brain is zinging. I did something good. No, better than good. Something amazing. I was in the movie. I saved the movie.

And all I had to do was apologize, have a great idea, wear a dress— and stand still for the longest five minutes of my life.